Caillou

Gets the Hiccups

Adaptation of the animated series: Sarah Margaret Johanson
Illustrations: Eric Sévigny, based on the animated series

chouette **dhx** media

Caillou and his family were enjoying a spaghetti dinner.
"Yum, spaghetti is my favorite," Caillou said.
"That's good, Caillou," Mommy said. "Please
try not to slurp when you eat."
It was very hard to eat the
spaghetti without slurping.
While Caillou was trying not
to slurp, he made a noise.
"Hiccup!"

"Uh-oh, sounds like you've got the hiccups," Daddy said.
"The hiccups? How do I stop them?" Caillou asked.
"Hiccups usually go away on their own," Mommy said.
Caillou waited a minute.
"Hiccup! Hey, I waited, but they didn't go away."
"You have to wait longer than that," Mommy explained. "Why not play in the living room?"

Caillou built a tower out of blocks while he waited.
But a hiccup made him knock over the tower.
"How's it going out here?" Mommy asked.
"These hiccups are messing up everything! Hiccup!
I need them to go away." Caillou said.
"Sometimes hiccups can be cured by giving someone
a scare," Mommy said.

"A scare?" Caillou said.

"Just a little scare. It makes the person gasp, and the hiccups go away. Do you want to give it a try?" Mommy asked.

"If it'll make my hiccups go away, then okay. Hiccup!" Caillou said.

Mommy spread her arms out and floated like a ghost, and then jumped at Caillou.

"Boo!" Mommy said.

"Hey, it worked," Caillou said.

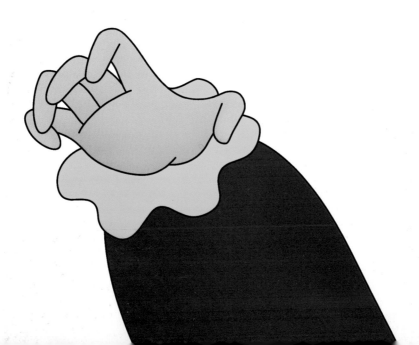

"Hiccup! Aw, it's not working," Caillou
said. "I don't think my hiccups are the
kind that get scared away. Hiccup!"
"Good thing I'm here, then," Daddy
said. "I'm the world's number one,
all-time hiccup cure champion. C'mon,
I'll show you."
Caillou and Daddy head outside.

"Some people cure hiccups by drinking water really fast from a hose! It can get a little messy," Daddy said.
"I don't care. Hiccup! I want to try."
Daddy turned on the water. Caillou tried to drink from the hose, but most of it sprayed all around.
"'Hiccup! It didn't work," Caillou said.
Daddy turned the hose off.

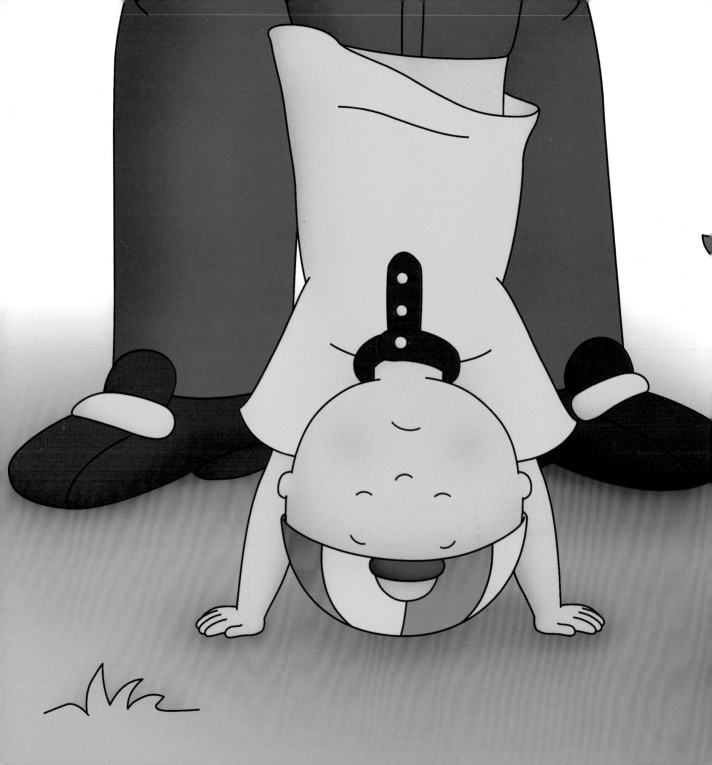

"Don't worry, Caillou. I've got another cure up my sleeve," Daddy said. "The upside-down solution always works!" Daddy made Caillou do a handstand so he was upside-down. Daddy held Caillou's feet for balance.

"Hiccups all gone?" Rosie asked.

Caillou hiccupped, then shook his head no.

"There's one more thing we can try!" Daddy wasn't giving up. "Let's go inside."

"I've saved the best for last," Daddy said. "This is sure to get rid of your hiccups."
"What is it? Hiccup!" Caillou asked, eagerly.
"You hop on your left foot, and rub your head with your right hand," Daddy explained, showing Caillou. Caillou thought Daddy looked silly hopping around. And so did Mommy and Rosie.

Caillou really wanted to get rid of his hiccups. So he started hopping, too.
"That's it, Caillou," Daddy said. "Hop those hiccups away."
Caillou stopped and said dramatically, "I'm still hiccupping! What if I have them forever? Hiccup! And ever and EVER!"

"Maybe I'll have to stop making spaghetti dinners," Mommy said, shaking her head.

Caillou gasped. "But spaghetti's my favorite, and Rosie's, and Daddy's, too," Caillou said.

"It wasn't the spaghetti that gave me the hiccups. I know it wasn't and besides I think they're gone. Listen."

Caillou was right. His hiccups had gone away.

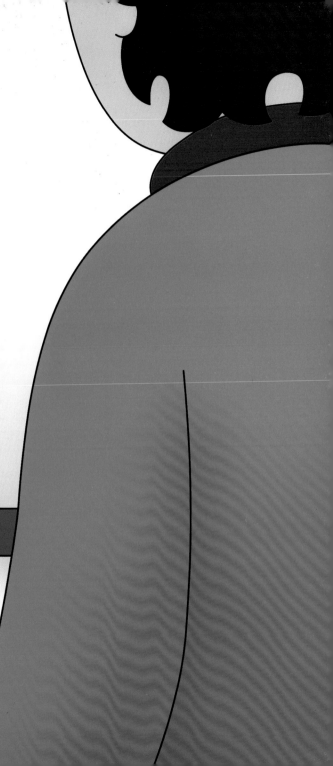

"Perhaps I scared them away by saying I wouldn't make spaghetti anymore?" Mommy suggested.
"No, I think they went away on their own, just like you said they would. But are you really going to stop making spaghetti?" Caillou asked in a very serious tone.
"Of course not, Caillou. I was just teasing," Mommy assured him.

Text: adaptation by Sarah Margaret Johanson of the animated series CAILLOU,
produced by DHX Media Inc.
All rights reserved.
Original story written by Kenn Scott
Original Episode # 508: Caillou's Hiccups
Illustrations: Eric Sévigny, based on the animated series CAILLOU
Art Direction: Monique Dupras

The PBS KIDS logo is a registered mark of PBS and is used with permission.

We acknowledge the financial support of the Government of Canada through
the Canada Book Fund for our publishing activities.

Canadian   Patrimoine
Heritage   canadien

We acknowledge the support of the Ministry of Culture and Communications
of Quebec and SODEC for the publication and promotion of this book.
SODEC
Québec

Bibliothèque et Archives nationales du Québec and Library and Archives
Canada cataloguing in publication

Johanson, Sarah Margaret, 1968-
Caillou gets the hiccups
(Clubhouse)
For children 3 years and up.

ISBN 978-2-89718-063-8

1. Hiccups - Juvenile literature. I. Sévigny, Éric. II. Title. III. Series: Clubhouse.
RC801.J63 2013   j616.3'3   C2013-940785-5

Printed in China
10 9 8 7 6 5 4 3 2 1   CHO1882 MAY2013